7/21

Ashford Library

AF → CA

For my nephew, Wayne.
Special thanks to my agent Helen, editors Emily and Grace,
and designer Lorna for making this book happen. — C.W.

First published 2021 by Macmillan Children's Books
an imprint of Pan Macmillan
The Smithson, 6 Briset Street, London EC1M 5NR
Associated companies throughout the world
www.panmacmillan.com

Hardback ISBN: 978-1-5290-4128-6
Paperback ISBN: 978-1-5290-4127-9

1 3 5 7 9 8 6 4 2

A CIP catalogue record for this book is available from the British Library.
Printed in China

MIX
Paper from
responsible sources
FSC® C116313
FSC
www.fsc.org

Cindy Wume

The Bookshop Cat

Macmillan Children's Books

There once was a black cat.
He came from a long line of very important cats.

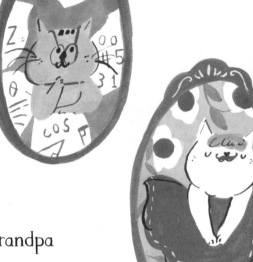

His grandma
was a well-known
mouse catcher.

His grandpa
had been a
famous dancer,

and his parents were the best
pastry chefs in the city!

His brothers and sisters all
had jobs they loved and
which kept them very busy.

But the black cat simply loved reading.

"Reading isn't a job," said his brother,
who was a mechanic. "Why not
pick up a spanner and join me?"

"Cooking is useful *and* fun,"
said his mum and dad. "You
could always work with us!"

"We love playing music," said his sisters. "Why don't you join our band?"

But the black cat just wanted to read.

"With a book, I can go anywhere and be anything," he replied.

The next morning, the black cat
set off to find a quiet reading spot.

He leapt aboard his usual bus,
opened his book, and began to purr.

He loved exploring the city, almost as much as he loved books.
Everywhere he looked there was something new and interesting.
And this particular morning he saw something very interesting indeed . . .

It was a lovely little bookshop
with a sign outside that read,

HELP WANTED.

His tail flicked with excitement.
If there was ever a job that
was made for him, this was it.

"It's perfect!" he cried.

"Perfect for what?" came a voice.
The poor little cat jumped out of his skin!

"Perfect for me," he replied. "I love
books and I would love to help."

"You'd better come in then," said the girl.

The girl was called Violet and the bookshop was for children.

"It has been in my family for many years," she explained. "I help my grandfather whenever I can, but we do need an extra hand."

"Well I have paws," replied the cat. "Maybe I can help."

And so, the very next morning, the black cat arrived,
bright and early, for his new job as – the Bookshop Cat.

They started by cleaning and tidying the shop.

They reordered the shelves, made new
displays and ordered lots of books.

They even placed a comfy armchair
in the sunny spot in the corner.

BUSINESS
FOR
CATS

"It's everything I could ever dream of!" sighed the Bookshop Cat
as he swished his tail with excitement and purred his loudest purr.

"Welcome!" said Violet, as the first customers arrived.

"All you could ever want is right here on these shelves," added the Bookshop Cat.

"We have books about animals and books about oceans. Books that will take you on adventures far away, where you will meet astronauts, villains and unicorns!"

Then he set about helping each and
every child to find the perfect book.

Before long, everyone in town
knew about the Bookshop Cat, and the
Children's Bookshop became busier than ever!

But one morning, the bus didn't come!

"The bus has broken down
because of the rain," said the birds.
"And they can't seem to fix it."

So the Bookshop Cat had to find a new way to get to work.

And, when he finally arrived, what a sight met his eyes!

"Quick, come and help!" shouted Violet.
"A pipe has burst! And the books are getting wet!"

The street had flooded and there was water everywhere.

With so much water to wade through, nobody
came into the shop that day. Or the day after . . .

Or the day after that!

The bookshop itself seemed to sigh with sadness.

"I think we've been forgotten," sniffed Violet.
But the Bookshop Cat said nothing.
He just curled up quietly in a corner.

He didn't even feel like reading.
In fact, he hadn't read a book in days!

And when news of this reached
the Bookshop Cat's family, they
knew something had to be done.

"Don't worry my dear," said his mum. "We're all here to help,
because that's what families are for. Just tell us what can we do."

And, very quietly, the Bookshop Cat began to purr.
Then Violet said. "I think I have an idea."

"If the children can't come to us, let's take the books to them."

And so, early the next morning, Violet, the Bookshop Cat and his family set off across the city.

They placed books in the playgrounds and along the beach. They put them on benches, in doctors' waiting rooms, inside the museum and the city aquarium. They even put books in the greengrocers, right next to the bananas!

When the children found the books they were so excited.
But Violet's plan was still unfolding, as tucked into the
back of each story was a note and a map.

Your adventures
are just beginning!

Follow the
map to find
out more ...

The children followed the map,
through the city, all the way to ...

. . . the Children's Bookshop, which had never looked more beautiful.
As the children rushed forward, the bookshop itself seemed to sigh with happiness.

The Bookshop Cat swished his tail with
excitement and purred his loudest purr.

If you visit the bookshop today, you'll see it's busy — very busy indeed!

And so is everyone else! Especially the Bookshop Cat, who helps every child find the perfect book.

STORY
TIME

10:00
4:00

The children still love reading,
now more than ever. Because,
thanks to the Bookshop Cat, they
know something very important.

That, with a book, you can go
anywhere and be anything!

The Bookshop Cat loves his job, and if you
happen to pass by, then stop and listen.

You're sure to hear a loud, contented purr coming from inside.